USBORNE

DRAWING
PEOPLE

USBORNE HOTSHOTS

DRAWING PEOPLE

Edited by Judy Tatchell
Designed by Ruth Russell

Illustrated by Roger Fereday, Derek Brazell, Kevin Lyles,
Chris West, Nicky Dupays, Howard Tangye, Lynne Robinson,
David Downton, Paddy Mounter and Graham Round

Cover illustration by Kathy Ward
Photography by Ray Moller

Based on material by
Alastair Smith
and Susan Meredith

CONTENTS

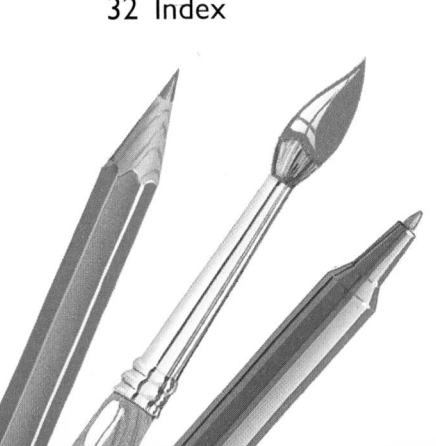

Before you start

It is easier to draw people if you have a real person, or a clear photograph, to copy from. Keep looking at the person or photograph as you draw. The more you look, the better your picture is likely to be.

Here are some different materials you could use for your pictures.

Watercolors

You can create different effects with watercolors by varying the amount of water you use. Use a little water for strong, vivid colors and more water for a softer effect.

Wet watercolor paints will blend together on the paper. Let a color dry before you add a new one next to it, unless you want the colors to blend.

Gouache

Gouache paint creates solid-looking, strong colors. It comes in tubes or jars. You can use it as it is, or mix it with water for a softer look.

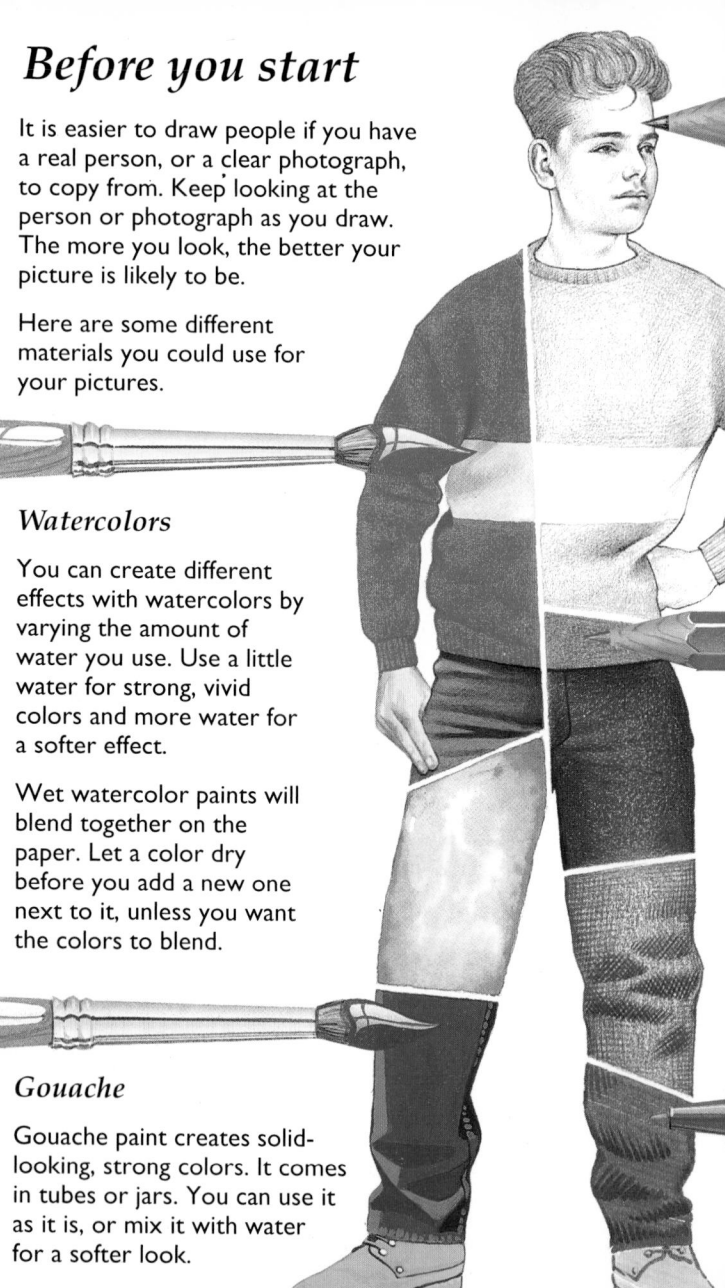

Pencils

Pencils are marked with a number and a letter to show how hard (H) or soft (B for black) they are. A medium hard (2H) pencil will mark paper easily but will not smudge. A softer pencil can be useful for dark shading. HB pencils are midway between hard and soft.

Colored pencils

Colored pencils come in a huge variety of shades. They do not smudge and by varying the pressure on the pencil, you can vary the depth of color. Pencils need to be sharp to draw details, and blunter for shading large areas.

Felt-tip pens

Felt-tip pens make bright, flat tones which are good for cartoon drawings.

Paper

For drawing practice, you can use any type of paper or sketch book. You can, though, buy special types of paper to suit the materials you are using.

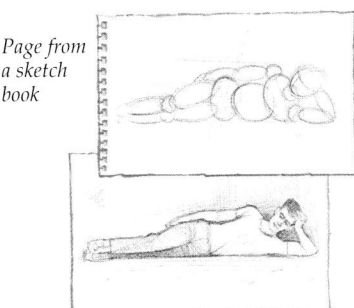

Page from a sketch book

Cartridge paper is cheap and smooth. It is good for use with colored pencils or felt-tip pens.

Watercolor paper

You need fairly thick paper for watercolor or gouache paints. You can buy thick cartridge paper, or use special watercolor paper. This comes in three textures: HP (smooth), NOT (slightly rougher) and Rough.

Heads and faces

Follow the steps shown here to draw a realistic-looking face. You can either copy these pictures or use a real person as a model. Start by sketching an oval, in pencil. Then draw some faint guidelines on it, called construction lines.

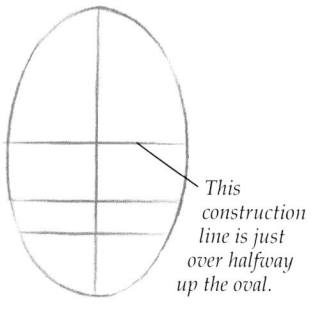

This construction line is just over halfway up the oval.

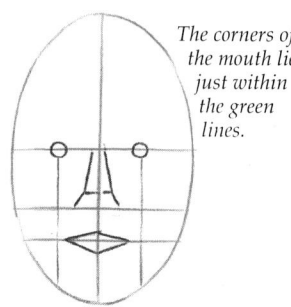

The corners of the mouth lie just within the green lines.

Draw a construction line down from the middle of each eye. Sketch features, using the construction lines as guides.

Draw the hair as a single shape.

The eyes are usually about one eye's width apart.

Work on the shapes of the features, and sketch in the outline of the hair. Keep your pencil lines light and soft.

The darkest part of the mouth is where the lips meet.

Shade lightly over the hair and face. Build up the shape by adding more layers, especially in areas which are in shadow.

Add dark swirls to the hair.

Show the eyelashes as a soft, dark line, rather than as individual lashes.

Leave the parts of the face and hair that catch the light with only one or two thin layers of color on them.

Instead of drawing hard outlines around features, give them shape by adding deeper shadows around them.

From start to finish, remember to keep looking at the person you are drawing. Only draw what you see.

You can keep on shading the face just by adding more thin layers of the same color. In areas of deep shadow, add darker shades. You can add touches of black to the darkest parts, such as inside the nostrils and parts of the hair.

Drawing from different angles

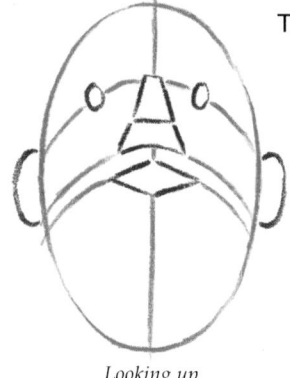

Looking up

The drawings on this page show you how to vary the positions of construction lines so that you can draw heads from different angles, and still get the features in the right places.

Curving the lines

For heads looking different ways, you may need to curve the construction lines. For instance, on a head looking up, the construction lines that cross the face need to be curved up.

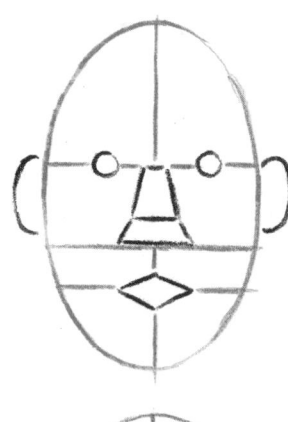

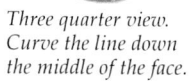

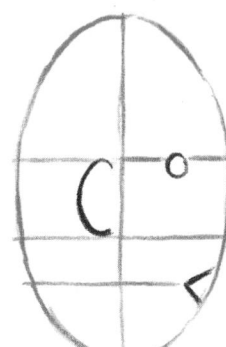

Three quarter view. Curve the line down the middle of the face.

Profile. The ears go just behind the construction line down the middle.

A drawing to try

Can you figure out how to draw a face looking up and to one side? Try mapping out the construction lines, combining the middle picture above and the picture at the top of the page. Tilt the oval head shape as well, to show the face looking up.

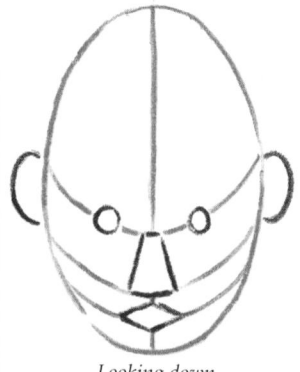

Looking down

Sketching practice

Drawing realistic-looking features isn't easy, especially if you want to draw them from different angles. For practice, try sketching different features on their own, quickly and roughly. If you mess it up, just start again on a new version.

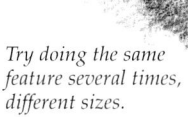

Try doing the same feature several times, different sizes.

Eyes are often what someone looks at first in a picture.

Do lots of mouths making different expressions.

Cameos

Cameos are silhouettes of heads drawn in profile.

First, sketch a head shape and add construction lines. Then plot the shape of the face and hair.

When the shape is accurate, go over the outline cleanly with a fine felt-tip pen. Erase any pencil sketch marks.

Fill in the shape, using black paint or felt-tip pen. For the finished effect, cut out an oval around the silhouette.

A sketchy style

This shows a less realistic, more glamorized style. It is best to base pictures like these on people with strong makeup or hairstyle. This picture was done using pencils and oil pastels, which make bold marks. You could use pencils, black chalk on white paper (or *vice versa*), or try it in color using colored pencils and chalks.

The first stage was done by imagining the rough shapes and shading around them. If you need to sketch in the shapes, do so lightly. It won't matter if they show a little, in a sketchy style such as this.

Try to imagine the rough shapes of the head. Shade in with soft pencil (6, 7 or 8B) or pale chalk.

Add the outline and define the features with a sharp, soft pencil or a sharp chalk.

Completing the picture

Use mid-grey to add tone and depth to the hair – you could smudge black and white chalk together. Add a little dark color to the lips, nails and earrings. Use soft pencil or the side of a small piece of chalk for the background. Leave a narrow white band around the head to prevent the background from looking too heavy.

Drawing bodies

The key to drawing a whole figure successfully is to do a good rough sketch first. This means working out the body shapes and positions in pencil before you finalize anything.

How many heads?

You need to get the body in proportion. This means getting the size of one part right compared to another. It helps to see how many head lengths make up the total height.

Men: about seven heads tall.

Women: about six-and-a-half heads tall.

Mid-teenagers: about six heads tall.

Four-year-olds: about three-and-a-half heads tall.

Rough sketches

To do a rough sketch, first sketch the rounded shapes of the head, chest, stomach and hips. Then add the limb shapes and draw the outline of the clothes. Don't erase mistakes. Just continue sketching lightly, improving the shapes as you go.

It is easier to work big rather than small.

Movement

Movement is difficult to capture in a drawing. Base your drawing on a photograph, or ask someone to keep repeating a simple movement for you.

Simple, bold, flowing lines can give a better feeling of action than a detailed drawing. You will still need to do a rough sketch to help you get the proportions right.

Rough sketch

Simple, bold, line drawing.

Collage

The line drawing above was used in a collage (see right). Simple shapes were cut out and stuck down, and the black line added on top.

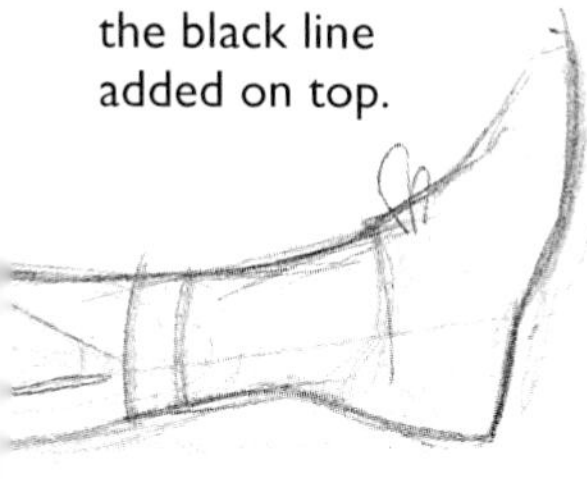

This picture is made by cutting up pieces of paper and sticking them down in the shape of a person.

The paper shapes are simpler than the black line shapes.

A patch of green paper, torn rather than cut out to give it a soft edge, suggests the background.

Portraits

Ask your model to pose in an interesting position.

A portrait is a picture of a real person. You could base a portrait on a photograph, or draw someone when they are sitting still – reading or watching television, for instance. Make sure your model is comfortable and don't expect them to pose for more than 15 minutes without a break.

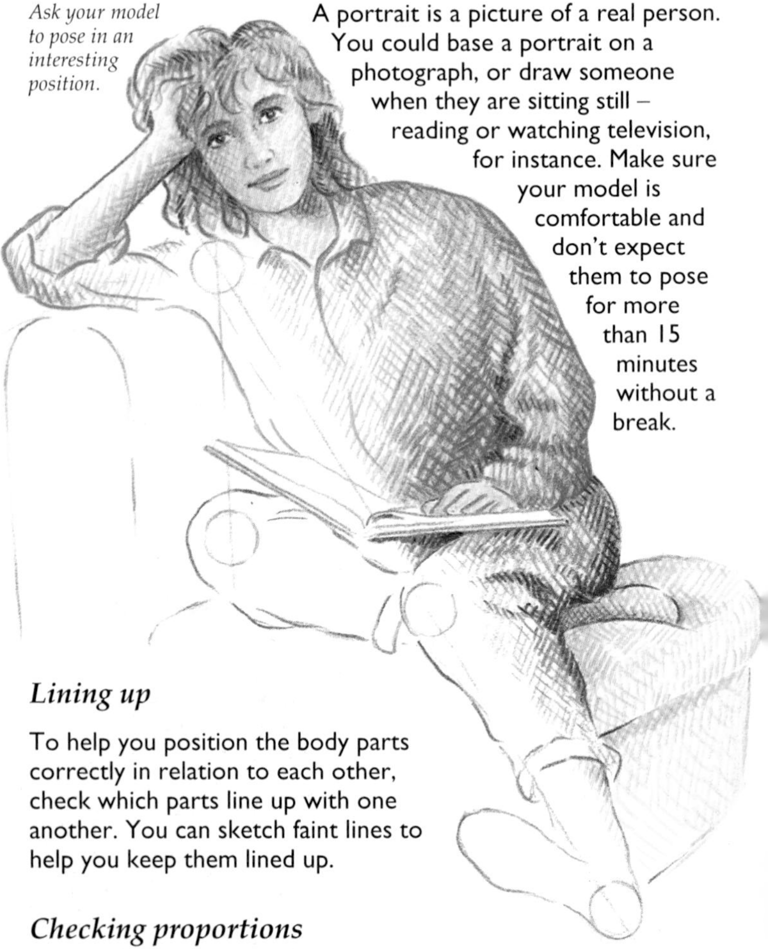

Lining up

To help you position the body parts correctly in relation to each other, check which parts line up with one another. You can sketch faint lines to help you keep them lined up.

Checking proportions

To help work out the proportions, shut one eye, then measure your model's head with a pencil held at arm's length, as shown on the right.

Use the head measurement to see how many head lengths make up the rest of the body, as shown in this picture.

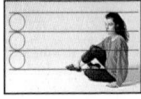

14

Lighting

If you are drawing a portrait from life, you can experiment with lighting to create different effects. Move an angle-poise lamp around to see where shadows appear and what effects you get.

The dramatic effect in this picture is created by shining a single light on the model, from the side.

This shows how the lighting was set up to shine on the model.

You could use black and white with tones of grey, as in this picture.

Build up the portrait gradually, looking for areas of light and shade.

Coloring in

Colored pencils, as used here, are good for coloring and shading because you can easily control the amount of color they make, by pressing lightly or firmly.

Shading

Shading gives shape. Look for light and shadow before you begin coloring. Leave white highlights blank, but shade the rest with pale color. Build up the shape by adding deeper shades.

Clothes

Shadows form on clothes where folds dip inward. There are highlights where folds catch the light. Most highlights and shadows are curved because of the shape of the body.

Hatching

Hatching is a shading technique often used with pencils, pens or colored pencils. It was used in the picture above to build up color and areas of shade.

Diagonal strokes, far apart for faint shading, closer together for stronger color.

Warm or cold?

Colors are sometimes described as cold or warm. For example, blues and greys are associated with cold things, such as steel or the sea. Oranges, yellows and reds are associated with warm things, such as fire and the sun.

You can create different atmospheres by your choice of colors. You could trace this picture twice and color one version entirely in warm colors and one in cold, to see the difference.

The girl's coat opposite is colored in a warm red to make it look more cozy.

Don't forget shadows under people's feet. This makes them look as if they are standing on the ground.

Cold colors

Warm colors

For deepest color, try crosshatching. Crisscross the strokes close together.

Hatching colors together can create a new color. This looks most effective from a distance.

Perspective and foreshortening

Here are two general drawing techniques which are useful to know about whatever you wish to draw. The techniques are known as drawing in perspective, and foreshortening.

Perspective

Drawing scenes in perspective means drawing them how you see them, so that things look smaller the farther away they are. The point at which something becomes so small that you can't see it is called the vanishing point.

Vanishing point

Sketching this scene

Start by drawing the vanishing point. Then draw guidelines, called disappearing lines, from this point. Sketch the rest of the scene using these guidelines.

Vanishing point

Disappearing lines

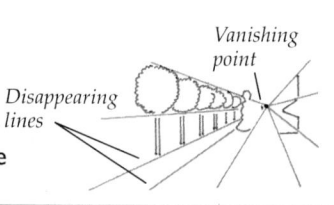

Foreshortening

The proportions of body parts can look distorted when drawn from certain angles. In this picture, the boots look bigger than the rest of the body and the body looks squashed. This effect is called foreshortening.

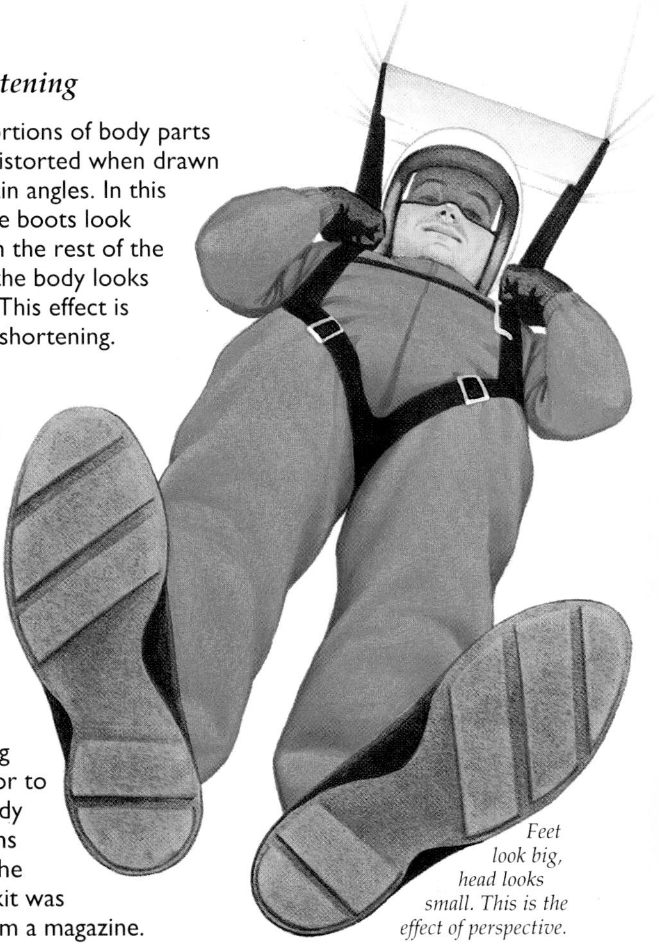

The body is foreshortened – drawn short and squashed.

The artist sat by the feet of a model lying on the floor to get the body proportions correct. The skydiving kit was copied from a magazine.

Feet look big, head looks small. This is the effect of perspective.

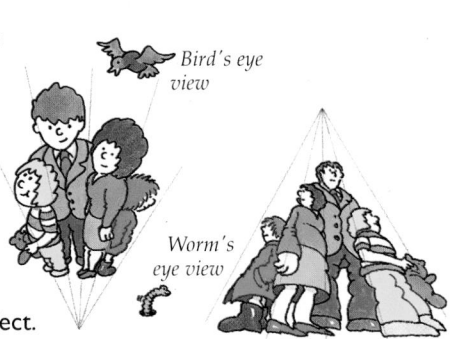

More dramatic views

Bird's eye and worm's eye views can make ordinary pictures look dramatic. Use disappearing lines to help get the people in perspective. You will need to foreshorten the bodies to get the right effect.

Bird's eye view

Worm's eye view

19

Cartoon faces

You may find cartoons easier to draw than realistic people, as the face and body shapes are simplified. Also, cartoons can look flat, with no complicated shading.

Faces

Draw a circle with two faint pencil lines crossing it.

Put the ears level with the nose in the middle.

Erase the lines before you color with felt-tip pens.

Expressions

You only need to add or change a few lines to create lots of different expressions in cartoon people.

The mouth and eyes create a fed-up look.

Put the nose and eyes high to leave room for the yawning mouth.

Exaggerate the mouth for laughter.

This sickly face has a greenish tinge.

The mouth and eyebrows make this person look glum.

Looking around

To draw a cartoon face looking to one side, follow the same principles as for a realistic face (see page 8). As the face looks to one side, the line going across the face stays level. The line going down the face curves in the direction in which the face is looking.

Front view　　*Starting to turn*　　*Turning farther*　　*Profile*

Looking up and down

To make a face look up or down, curve the line across it. The more the line curves, the higher up or lower down the person looks.

Looking up

Looking up more

Looking down

To make the face look both up and to one side, curve both lines that cross the face.

Cartoon bodies

You can add bodies to cartoon heads by first drawing a stick figure and then filling the body out around it. Keep the clothes simple and curve the edges to show the rounded shape of the body.

Sketching the clothes...

Sketching the stick figures...

Draw the stick figure lightly in pencil, so you can erase it later.

Draw the outline of the clothes in pencil starting at the neck and working down the figure.

Walking and running

The right arm is in front when the left leg is forward and *vice versa*. When someone walks, there is always one foot on the ground. When someone runs, there is a moment when both feet are off the ground.

Walking. One foot always on the ground.

Starting to run, the body leans forward and the elbows bend more.

Running fast. Both feet are off the ground.

Slowing down again.

22

Coloring in...

Go over the outline with a fine, dark felt-tip pen. The outline doesn't have to be black. Try a brown or dark blue for variety. Erase the stick shapes before you color the figures brightly.

Jumping

The faster someone runs, the more they lean forward and the farther the arms stretch. Jumping is like an exaggerated run. The arms stretch out behind and in front, and the legs spread even wider.

Running toward the jump.

The back leg bends to push off into the jump.

In mid-flight, arms and legs are at full stretch.

Both feet come forward to land.

Caricatures

A caricature is a picture of a person which exaggerates their most striking features. Although a caricature looks funny, you can still recognize the person. Caricatures have lots of expression, so it might be easier to draw from a lively photograph of someone, rather than asking them to hold an expression while you draw.

Original photo

1. Try to get a good, clear, simplified face shape first.

2. Position the features on the face, using guidelines.

3. Exaggerate the size and shape of the main features.

The things to exaggerate here are the hair, the shape of the eyes and the big smile.

Caricaturing tip

Before you start drawing a caricature, imagine the features you would pick out if you were describing to someone else what the person looks like. These are the features to exaggerate in your caricature.

Original photo

1. Do a face shape, positioning extras, such as glasses.

2. The arms and hands are important in this picture.

3. Exaggerate the shape of the mouth.

The forehead is higher than in real life.

The main features are the cheeks, the smile and the hair.

Glasses and hair accessories add interest to a caricature.

Fashion illustration

Fashion illustration is a way of showing clothes so that they look attractive and glamorous. If you are interested in clothes and style, you will probably enjoy fashion illustration. Fashion models are usually drawn unrealistically tall and thin, to make the clothes look more elegant.

Watercolor illustration

First, do a pencil sketch of a posing model's body shapes. You could base your sketch on a photo of a real fashion model.

Sketch the figure again with longer limbs. Make the figure unnaturally long and slender. (With practice, you might be able to skip the stage above.)

Draw simplified outlines of clothes around the body sketch. Keep the outline sleek and flowing. Then use watercolor as shown.

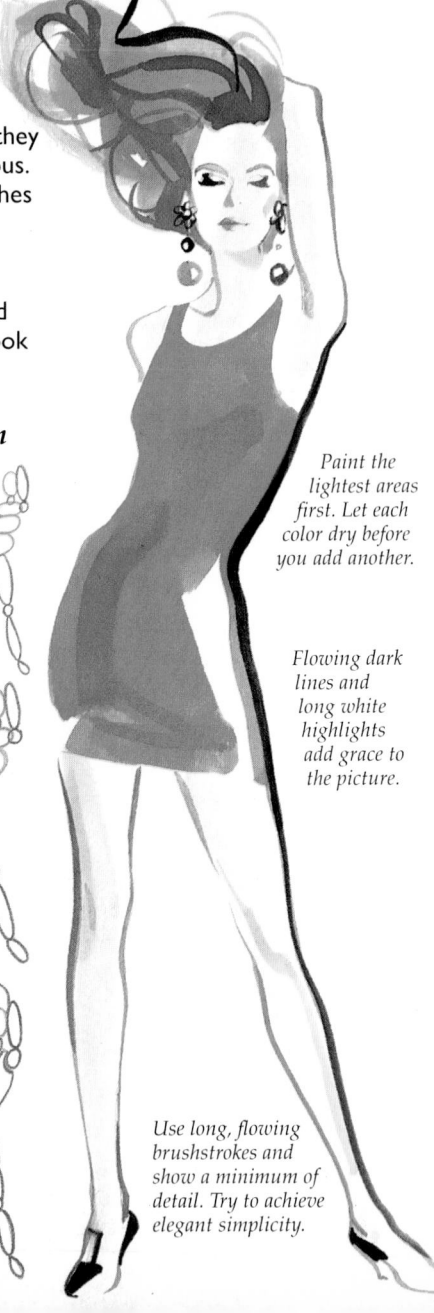

Paint the lightest areas first. Let each color dry before you add another.

Flowing dark lines and long white highlights add grace to the picture.

Use long, flowing brushstrokes and show a minimum of detail. Try to achieve elegant simplicity.

Pastel illustration

Pastels come in sticks, like chalks. They give a soft, bright effect and interesting textures, especially if you use them on fairly rough paper.

This picture was sketched following the stages described on the previous page. Then the shapes were blocked in with pastels, as shown below. The picture was then finished as shown on the right.

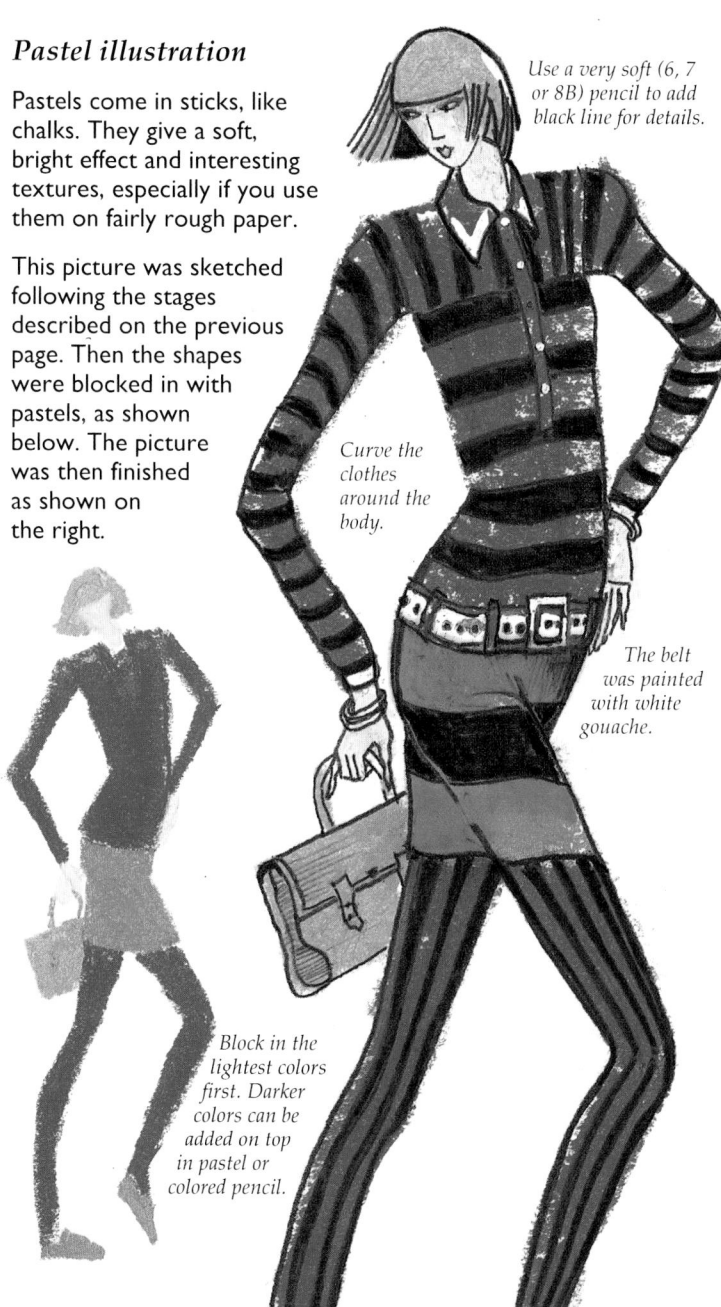

Use a very soft (6, 7 or 8B) pencil to add black line for details.

Curve the clothes around the body.

The belt was painted with white gouache.

Block in the lightest colors first. Darker colors can be added on top in pastel or colored pencil.

Mix and match people

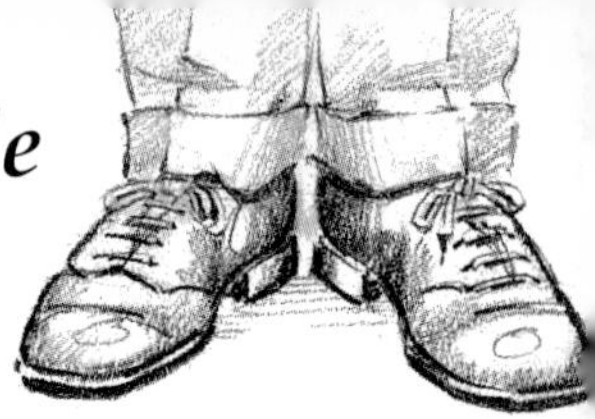

You can use these parts of people in your own pictures, or you could just try copying them separately, as shown here, for practice.

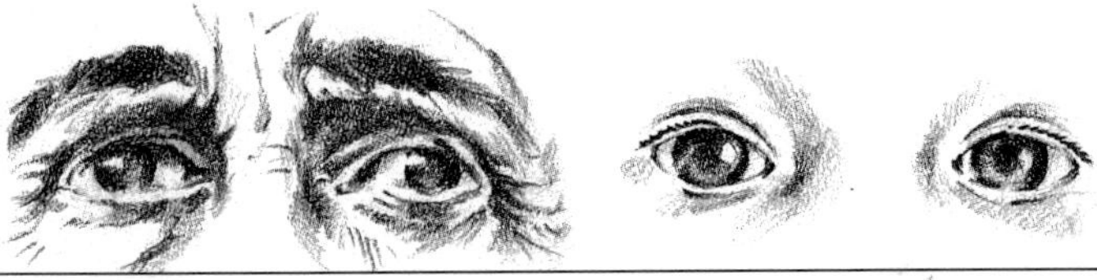

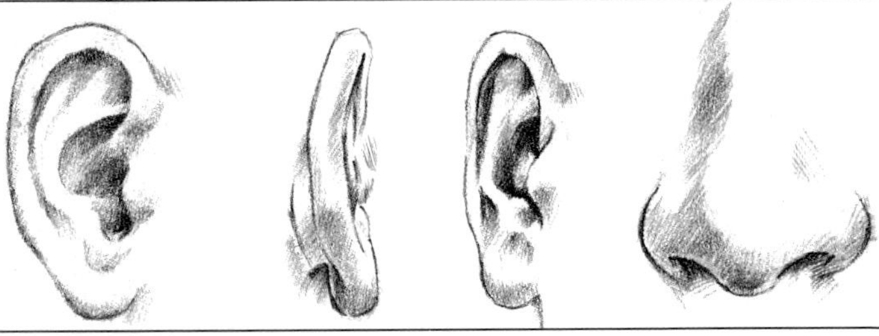

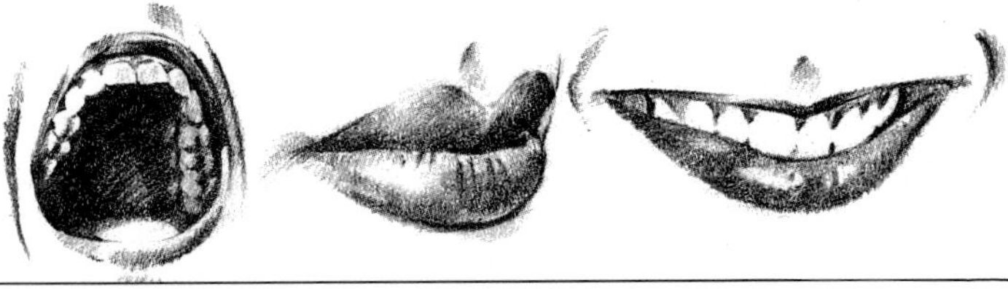

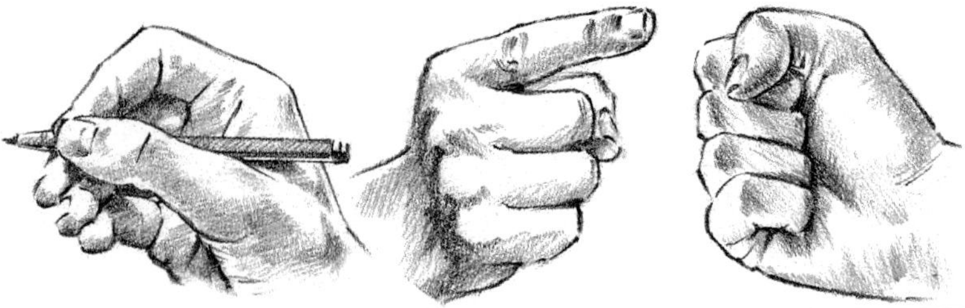

28

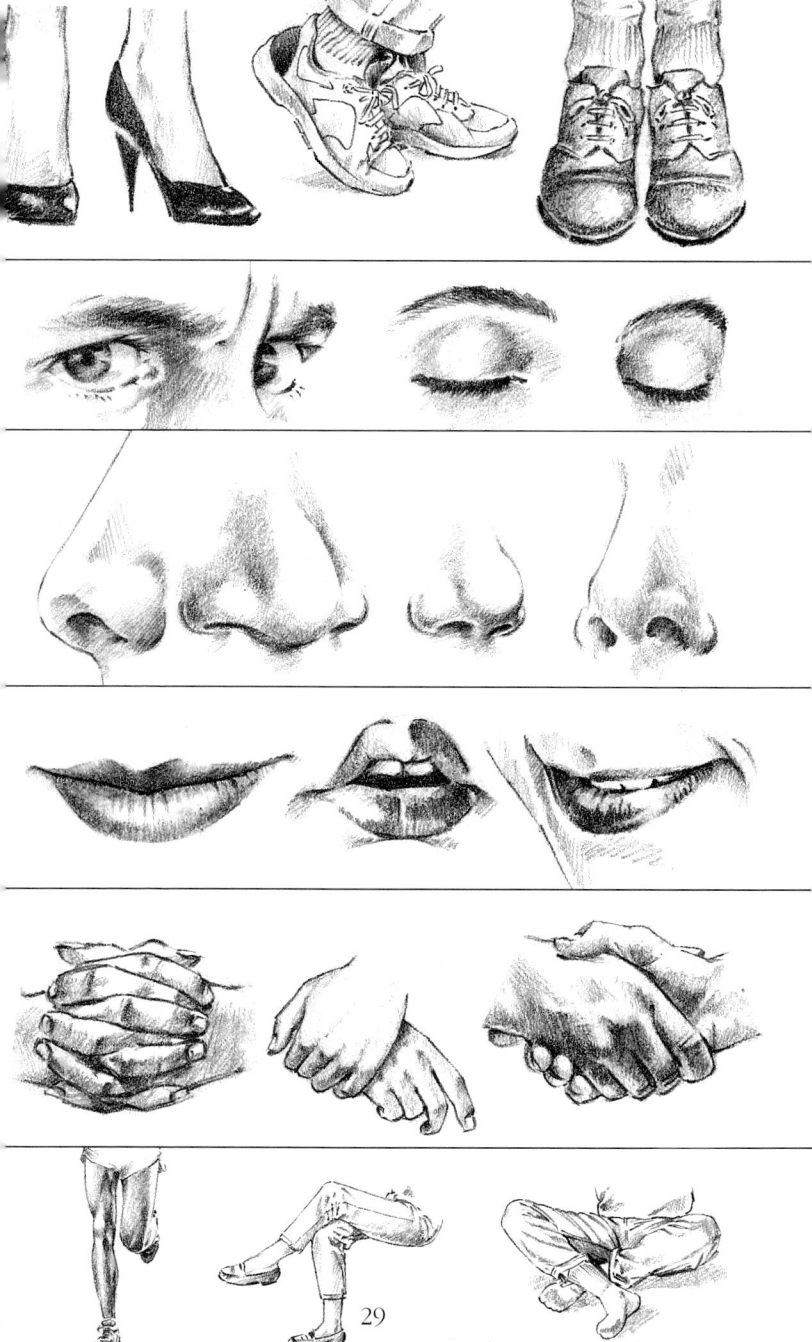

Cartoon bodies

Here are lots of pictures of cartoon heads, bodies and legs from different sides for you to use in your pictures. You can mix and match them, and color them in differently from how they are shown here.

A person's head might be facing you while the body is sideways.

Index

This book is based on material previously published in *How to Draw People, Usborne Guide to Fashion Design* and *The Usborne Complete Book of Drawing*.

First published in 1997 by Usborne Publishing Ltd, Usborne House, 83-85 Saffron Hill, London EC1N 8RT, England. First published in America August 1997. AE